This book belongs to:

Mia and Milo

I Love You, Mommy and Daddy

Written by Jillian Harker
Illustrated by Kristina Stephenson

First published 2008 by Parragon Books, Ltd.
Copyright © 2018 Cottage Door Press, LLC
5005 Newport Drive, Rolling Meadows, Illinois 60008

All Rights Reserved

ISBN: 978-1-68052-424-6

Parragon Books is an imprint of Cottage Door Press, LLC.
Parragon Books® and the Parragon® logo are registered
trademarks of Cottage Door Press, LLC.

Contents

I Love You, Mommy

I Love You, Daddy

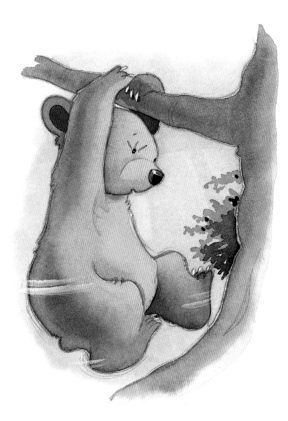

I Love You, Mommy

"Watch me, Mommy," called Little Bear.
"I'm going fishing."

"Wait a minute," replied Mommy Bear.
"There's something you might want to know."

But Little Bear was already
running down to the river.

11

Mommy Bear ran, too.

She saw Little
Bear jump onto
a rock.

She saw Little Bear
reach out his paw
to catch a fish.

Then Little Bear began to teeter and totter.

SPLASH!

"This doesn't feel so good!" thought Little Bear.

"Good try!" smiled Mommy Bear. "But you watch me now, Little Bear. I'll show you how to swim before you go fishing again." Little Bear watched Mommy Bear paddle all around.

"Your turn now, Little Bear," she said.

Little Bear did exactly what Mommy Bear had done.

"This feels good!" thought Little Bear.

"I love Mommy."

"Look at me, Mommy," called Little Bear.
"I'm going to pick that fruit."
"Just a minute," replied Mommy Bear.
"There's something you might want to know."

But Little Bear was
already climbing the tree.

Mommy Bear saw
Little Bear run
along a branch.

She saw Little Bear
reach out his paw to
pick a juicy fruit.

Then Little Bear began to *wibble* and *wobble*.

CRASH!

"This doesn't feel like fun!" thought Little Bear.

"Not bad!" said Mommy Bear. "But you look at me now, Little Bear. I'll show you how to climb properly before you go fruit-picking again."

Little Bear watched how Mommy Bear balanced as she climbed. "Your turn now, Little Bear," she said.

Little Bear did what Mommy Bear had done.
"This tastes good!" thought Little Bear.
"I love Mommy."

"Look, Mommy," smiled Little Bear. "All the other cubs are playing. I'm going to play, too."

"Wait a minute, please," said Mommy Bear. "There's something you might want to know."

Little Bear stopped and turned. "Tell me," he said.

"Be gentle when you play," said Mommy Bear.

"Look. Like this." Mommy Bear reached out her paws. She wrapped her arms around Little Bear. She rolled Little Bear over and over on the ground.

"I love Mommy," thought Little Bear. Then he ran off
to play. He did just what Mommy Bear had done.

And it felt like fun!

Little Bear was very tired when he got home,
but there was something he wanted to say.
"I wanted to tell you," said Little Bear.
"What?" asked Mommy Bear.

"I love you, M..."
But Little Bear didn't finish.

Mommy Bear kissed Little Bear's sleepy head.

"I love you, too," she said.

I Love You, Daddy

"You're getting tall, Little Bear," said Daddy Bear.
"Big enough to come climbing with me."
Little Bear's eyes opened wide in surprise.
   "Do you really mean that?" said Little Bear.
Daddy Bear nodded. He led Little Bear to
a giant tree.

Little Bear tried to scramble
up onto the lowest branch.

He tumbled backward.

Daddy Bear
nudged
Little Bear.

Daddy Bear
tugged Little
Bear.

"You can do it!" he whispered.

And suddenly, Little Bear found that he could. "I love Daddy," thought Little Bear.

"You're getting brave, Little Bear,"
said Daddy Bear. "Daring enough
to gather honey with me."
Little Bear gasped.

"Could I really?"
Daddy Bear winked.
He led Little Bear to
another tree and pointed
to a hole in the trunk.

Little Bear reached out his paw.
A furious buzzing filled his ears.
Little Bear pulled his paw back.

Buzz!

Buzz!

Buzz!

Buzz!

"Just be quick," Daddy Bear said. "You have thick fur. The bees can't hurt you. You can do it!" he smiled.

And suddenly, Little Bear found that he could.

"I love Daddy," thought Little Bear.

"You're getting smart, Little Bear.
Smart enough to find a good winter den."
Little Bear grinned.
"Do you really think so?"
"I know so," said Daddy Bear.

Little Bear set off.
"Not too far from food," said Daddy Bear.
"Ready for when spring comes."
Little Bear sniffed the wind.

"Look for high ground," said
Daddy Bear, "to keep us dry."
Little Bear padded up
over the rocks.

"Somewhere safe and
warm," said Daddy Bear,
"away from danger."

"Here!" called Little Bear as he
disappeared into a deep cave.

Daddy Bear followed. He looked all around.
"Perfect!" he said.
"I love Daddy," thought Little Bear.

"Did I climb well?" Little Bear asked on the way home.

"You did!" replied Daddy Bear.

"Was I brave?" asked Little Bear.

"You were!" answered Daddy Bear.

"Did I find a good den?" asked Little Bear.

"The very best!" smiled Daddy Bear. "I'm proud of you, Little Bear."

Soon Little Bear and Daddy Bear reached home.
And suddenly, Little Bear felt very tired,
but there was something he wanted to say.

"I love you, D..." began Little Bear.
But he didn't finish.

Daddy Bear stroked Little Bear's head.
"I love you, too," he said.

The End